If You Were My Valentine

Written by **Lynn Plourde** ✦ Illustrated by **Jennifer L. Meyer**

LITTLE, BROWN AND COMPANY

New York   Boston

About This Book

The illustrations for this book were done in pencil, then painted digitally in Photoshop. This book was edited by Deirdre Jones and designed by Patrick Collins with art direction from Saho Fujii. The production was supervised by Lillian Sun, and the production editor was Marisa Finkelstein. The text was set in Horley Old Style MT, and the display type was hand-lettered by David Coulson.

For Kolbi, who melts our hearts
—LP

May you have many
loving and beautiful moments to cherish!
—JLM

If you were my valentine,

I would jump, jump with joy.

If you were my valentine,

I would snuggle your shivers away.

If you were my valentine,
I would share the grandest
views with you.

If you were my valentine,

I would play

hide-and-seek-and-peek

with you.

If you were my valentine,

I would make your day sweeter than sweet.

If you were my valentine.

I would share hidden treasures with you.

If you were my valentine,

I would soar high in the sky to share a message with you.

If you were my valentine,
I would lean in until our love becomes one.

If you were my valentine,
I would announce it with a bigger-than-big

splash!

If you were my valentine,

I would rustle and tussle and tumble with you.

If you were my valentine,

I would hold you until you drifted off to dreamland.

If you were my valentine,

I would stay up all night with you.

If you were my valentine,
I would catch the moon
and the stars for you.

If you were my valentine,
there's something
you should hear.

You would be my valentine…

...EVERY day of the year.